The Tale of the Great Bunny

The Story of the Magical Underground World of Chocolate

Based on a story by
Krystyna Lagowski

Adapted by
Sarah Clarke

Illustrated by
Ron Berg

Published by
Alpha Corporation
Toronto, Canada

Story by: Krystyna Lagowski
Adapted by: Sarah Clarke
Illustrations: Ron Berg
Publishing Consultant: Alpha Corporation, a subsidiary of
                       Alpha Communications Corp.

Printed and Bound in Canada

I can barely remember my first visit to the children with chocolate gifts on Easter morning, it was so long ago.

In some of the houses that I visit children have left me a letter or drawn a picture of what they think I look like and where I live. Perhaps you have spotted my chocolate egg trails on Easter morning and wondered how they got there.

I hope that you will enjoy learning about my magical land where the chocolate grows.

I will be thinking of you, not just on this Easter day, but for every year to come.

love from– Great Bunny

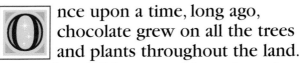

Once upon a time, long ago, chocolate grew on all the trees and plants throughout the land. Everyday children would run into the fields and woods to pick the chocolate flowers and fruits. They tasted delicious.

Great Bunny and his animal friends used to hide away to watch the children fill their baskets to the very top. They nibbled chocolate bark and leaves as they gathered chocolate to take home to share with their brothers and sisters.

As you can imagine everyone was very happy.

Can you see how many chocolate flowers the children have picked?

Then, one sad day, the magic was blown away and the chocolate trees began to disappear. In their place trees and bushes with strange fruits grew and from the ground came green grass instead of chocolate flowers. Great Bunny knew that if he was going to save chocolate he would have to take some back to a magical land, deep under the ground.

Do you like chocolate?

Luckily the children of long ago really loved chocolate. When Great Bunny asked for their help they collected as many of the chocolate eggs that had fallen from the trees as they could find.

Soon Great Bunny had enough eggs to begin his journey and he set off with his friend B.B. the Beaver.

Great Bunny and B.B. made their way through the tunnels and caves under the ground back to the secret magic land. It was very dark and there were many tunnels, so they laid a trail of eggs to help them find their way back.

How many eggs can you see?

Down and down they went, twisting and turning this way and that. Their torch was burning low and the bag of eggs on Great Bunny's back began to feel heavier and heavier. They had almost given up hope of finding their way out of the tunnel when they caught sight of a faint light around the next corner.

At last they had found it!! The special place where magic makes chocolate grow.
B.B. took his spade and set about planting the eggs that the children had saved.
No sooner had the eggs touched the earth than tall chocolate trees sprung up.
Before very long B.B. and Great Bunny were surrounded.

There were not only chocolate trees with chocolate eggs growing on, but chocolate houses too. Great Bunny named this land, "The Land of Cadbury".

Word of this enchanted chocolate land quickly spread among all the other animals. Soon Great Bunny and B.B. had many new friends helping them to gather the chocolate.

How many animals can you see in this picture?

One day, Great Bunny was looking out across this chocolate land from one of the turrets of Cadbury Castle. He caught sight of a faint purple glow coming from one of the caves beneath the castle itself. That night, while everyone was sleeping, he crept down to the secret cave and peeped inside.

A beautiful golden chest lay on the rough stone floor. Inside were the most special chocolates of all, Wishing Eggs. Way back in the days when chocolate had only just started to grow Great Bunny had heard about these Wishing Eggs but had never actually seen one. Now that he had found them he knew that it was time to share them with those who had helped him to save chocolate.

Can you guess who?

That's right, Great Bunny wanted to share
his chocolate with all the children.
Soon everyone was busy helping to make
chocolate treats for the children.
The badgers gathered all the chocolate
they could find.

The rabbits painted the eggs and
made wonderful chocolate
shapes. They even made one of
the Great Bunny himself
holding a Purple Wishing Egg.
He had to stand still for a very
long time so that they could get the shape
just right. B.B. and his Beaver friends
gathered the eggs from the trees and
wrapped them in brightly coloured paper.

All the animals had to work very fast to
get everything ready in time for Easter
morning.

When everything was ready Great Bunny packed his basket himself, to make sure that every treat was perfect. He marked each gift with his purple paw-print, so that the children would know that it came from the magic Land of Cadbury and the Great Bunny.

Finally, after much rushing around and a lot of hard work, the basket was full to the very top with delicious chocolate surprises. Great Bunny set off on his journey back through the twisting tunnels to take his gifts to the children.

"Wobbling Whiskers" said Great Bunny
"It's nearly dawn however shall I get the
treats to all the children now?".

He need not have worried. As he drew near
to the houses he could think only of the
smiles of joy on the children's faces when
they saw their chocolate surprises. His steps
quickened and he no longer
noticed the weight of the basket
in his paws as he hopped
here and there.

Inside the houses it was still very dark and
all the children were tucked up in bed fast
asleep. In every house Great Bunny left a
trail of eggs to show him the way out.
In his haste he forgot to gather up some of
the eggs when he left. If you look carefully
on Easter morning you may still be able to
see them for yourself.

How many eggs has the
Great Bunny left in this picture?

When you wake up on Easter morning you will see that Great Bunny has left you some delicious treats. If you look carefully among these surprises you may find your very own chocolate Great Bunny.

All these gifts are Great Bunny's way of saying thank you to all of the children for helping him to save chocolate.

Great Bunny, B.B. and all of their friends want you to share in the magic of the Land of Cadbury, so remember to make a wish every time you eat a special Wishing Egg.

Everyone in the Land of Cadbury hopes that you have enjoyed reading this story and hearing about the Great Bunny and all his animal friends.

B.B. and his helpers are always busy under the ground planting chocolate in the magic fields and woods. They all like to see the children enjoying their chocolate treats.

Perhaps this year they will visit you. Keep watching for them and you may just catch a glimpse of B.B.'s bright red cap as he scurries along. If you're up very, very early on Easter morning who knows who you might see hopping from house to house leaving wonderful chocolate surprises as he goes...